JULIA DONALDSON · LYDIA MONKS

The Ladybird Heard

Story Play

The Characters

Narrator All animals Cow Hen Horse Hog

Goose Duck Sheep Dog Cat 1 Cat 2

Ladybird Farmer Hefty Hugh Lanky Len Policeman 1 Policeman 2

Macmillan Children's Books

Bringing the Story to Life

There are lots of ways you can enjoy this story play, whether you are reading it on your own, sharing it with a friend or acting it out in a group.

If you are reading on your own, why not try doing different voices for the characters? Can you whisper like the quiet little ladybird or miaow like the cats?

Read the story play aloud with someone else – maybe one of you could be the narrator and one could be the other characters.

Have fun sharing the story with a group of family or friends, dividing the parts between you. You might need to do a couple each if there aren't enough of you.

Try some acting, too. Think about how each animal moves – do they get around on two legs, or four? Do they have wings? Do they move fast or slowly?

You can even put on a play at home or in your classroom. You'll find extra instructions in grey that will give you ideas about how to act out the story.

Have a rehearsal with your fellow actors before the big performance. Learn your lines and practise as much as you can!

Try and find some props. How about hats for the policemen, a phone for the farmer and a torch and a key for Len and Hugh? You could even make your own map.

How to Draw a Ladybird

 Start by drawing a big semi-circle.

Divide your semi-circle in two with a curvy line. The part to the left of the line will be the ladybird's face and should be a bit smaller than the other part, which will be her body.

Draw two round eyes to the left of your line.

Now add a big smile underneath the eyes.

Draw two bendy antennae on top of the ladybird's head.

The ladybird needs six straight little legs. Draw them along the bottom of your semi-circle.

Finish off by adding two big spots on her body.

You can use black and red pens or pencils to colour in your ladybird. Why not cut her out and use sticky tape to attach her to a stick? That way you can use her as a puppet if you put on a play!

Animals take up their places in the farmyard,
herded in by the farmer.

 Once upon a farm lived a fat red hen,
A duck in a pond and a goose in a pen,
A woolly sheep, a hairy hog,
A handsome horse and a dainty dog,
A cat that miaowed and a cat that purred,
A fine prize cow...
And a ladybird.

 And the cow said

 MOO!

 and the hen said

 CLUCK!

 HISS!

 said the goose and

 QUACK!

 said the duck.

 NEIGH!

 said the horse.

 OINK!

 said the hog.

 BAA!

 said the sheep.

 WOOF!

 said the dog.
One cat miaowed

 MIAOW!

 while the other one purred,

PRRRRRRR!

And the ladybird said never a word.
But the ladybird saw,
And the ladybird heard . . .

Enter Hefty Hugh and Lanky Len. They mime driving a van, then stop and look at a map. One of them holds a big key (the key to the cow's shed).

She saw two men in a big black van,
With a map and a key and a cunning plan.
And she heard them whisper,

This is how
We're going to steal the fine prize cow:

Open the gate at dead of night.

Pass the horse and then turn right.

Round the duck pond, past the hog.

Be careful not to wake the dog.

Left past the sheep,

Then straight ahead

And in through the door of the prize cow's shed!

Hugh and Len mime driving away.

STAGE LIGHTS UP

 And the little spotty ladybird
(Who never before had said a word)
Told the animals,

 This is how
Two thieves are planning to steal the cow:
They'll open the gate at dead of night.
Pass the horse and then turn right.
Round the duck pond, past the hog
(Being careful not to wake the dog).
Left past the sheep, then straight ahead
And in through the door of the prize cow's shed!

And the cow said

 MOO!

 and the hen said

 CLUCK!

 HISS!

 said the goose and

 QUACK!

 said the duck.

 NEIGH!

 said the horse.

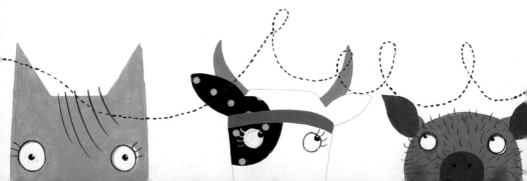

OINK!

 said the hog.

 BAA!

 said the sheep.

 WOOF!

 said the dog.
And both the cats began to miaow:

 MIAOW!

 We *can't* let them steal the fine prize cow!

 But the ladybird had a good idea
And she whispered it into each animal ear.

The ladybird whispers to all the animals.

At dead of night . . .

BLACKOUT
Enter Hugh and Len, on foot, creeping.
They have the map and key, and a torch.

 the two bad men
(Hefty Hugh and Lanky Len)
Opened the gate while the farmer slept
And *tiptoe* into the farm they crept.

*During the following section, Hugh and Len tiptoe round
the stage, following the trickster noises and so going
in the wrong direction.*

 Then the goose said

 NEIGH!

 with all her might.
And Len said,

 That's the horse – turn right.

The dainty dog began to

 QUACK!

 The duck!

 We must be right on track!

  OINK!

 said the cats.

 There goes the hog!

 Be careful not to wake the dog.

 BAA BAA BAA!

 said the fat red hen.

 The sheep! We're nearly there now, Len.

 Then the duck on the pond said

 MOO MOO MOO!

Just two more steps to go now, Hugh!

And they both stepped into the duck pond – SPLOSH!

Hugh and Len mime falling into the duck pond.
STAGE LIGHTS COME HALF UP
Enter Farmer, with phone.

 And the farmer woke and said

 Golly gosh!

 And he called the cops, and they came –

Enter two policemen, miming driving a car.

 NEE NAH!

 And they threw the thieves in their panda car.

The police mime bundling Hugh and Len into the
back of their car and driving off.

Then the cow said

 MOO!

 and the hen said

 CLUCK!

 HISS!

 said the goose and

 QUACK!

 said the duck.

 NEIGH!

 said the horse.

 OINK!

 said the hog.

BAA!

 said the sheep.

 WOOF!

 said the dog.
And the farmer cheered

 Hooray!

 and both cats purred,

  PRRRRRRR!

But the ladybird said never a word.

Well hello there! We are

Overjoyed that you have joined our celebration of

Reading books and sharing stories, because we

Love bringing books to you.

Did you know, we are a charity dedicated to celebrating the

On your bookmarks, get set, read!

Brilliance of reading for pleasure for everyone, everywhere?

Our mission is to help you discover brand new stories and

Open your mind to exciting worlds and characters, from

Kings and queens to wizards and pirates to animals and adventurers and so many more. We couldn't

Do it without all the amazing authors and illustrators, booksellers and bookshops, publishers, schools and libraries out there –

And most importantly, we couldn't do it all without . . .

You!

WORLD
**BOOK
DAY**

Changing lives through a love of books and shared reading.

World Book Day is a registered charity funded by publishers and booksellers in the UK & Ireland.

ILLUSTRATION *Rob Biddulph*